CHICKEN KARAOKE

By Heidi E. Y. Stemple

Illustrated by Aaron Spurgeon

Ready-to-Read

Simon Spotlight
New York   London   Toronto   Sydney   New Delhi

For Lexi
and all the booksellers
who get books
into the hands of readers
—H. E. Y. S.

To my daughter Jackie.
Have the courage
to use your voice
like the mother duck in this story.
—with love, Aaron

SIMON SPOTLIGHT

An imprint of Simon & Schuster Children's Publishing Division

1230 Avenue of the Americas, New York, New York 10020

This Simon Spotlight edition January 2023

Text copyright © 2023 by Heidi E. Y. Stemple

Illustrations copyright © 2023 by Aaron Spurgeon

All rights reserved, including the right of reproduction in whole or in part in any form.

SIMON SPOTLIGHT, READY-TO-READ, and colophon are registered trademarks of Simon & Schuster, Inc.

For information about special discounts for bulk purchases, please contact Simon & Schuster Special Sales at 1-866-506-1949 or business@simonandschuster.com.

Manufactured in the United States of America 1222 LAK

10 9 8 7 6 5 4 3 2 1

This book has been cataloged with the Library of Congress.

ISBN 978-1-6659-1390-4 (hc)

ISBN 978-1-6659-1389-8 (pbk)

ISBN 978-1-6659-1391-1 (ebook)

Duck arrives,
ducklings in tow.
She warms up her voice
with notes high
and notes low.

The sign on the door says
Chicken Karaoke Show!

"Cluck, cluck, cluck!
Come try your luck!"
A chicken hands
a number to Duck.

She looks around.
She is starstruck.

The flamingos are first.
The machine blares
their score.
They sing, sing, sing,
and sing some more.

Duck inches her way
back toward the door.

"Cluck, cluck, cluck."
A new number is called.
"Twenty-two! Twenty-two?

Hey you at the door—
twenty-two is you!"

Duck climbs up onstage,
grabs the mic
with her wing.

She can do this.
She can SING!

Her voice starts
a bit quack-y.
Her knees knock.
Her palms sweat.

But the crowd cheers
as she reaches
her highest note yet!
"Ooohhhhhhhhhhh!!!"

Oh no!
Cluck, cluck, cluck!
The machine runs amuck.

As Duck sings the high note,
her song is stuck!

Hold that note, Duck.
We will get it unstuck!

The hens and the rooster
all scramble around.
One lays an egg right there
on the ground.

Duck is still holding
that note way up high.
Her eyes start to water.
Her mouth is so dry.

The hens all push buttons.
Rooster grabs tools.
Toucan reads
the karaoke rules.

"Ahhhhhhhh!" sings Duck,
running out of air.

Crack—
comes a small sound
from under a chair.

YANK!

The crowd falls silent . . .

. . . then bursts into applause.
Toucan reads aloud the karaoke laws:

"'The winner is the singer who gets the most cheers,' and Duck has gotten the most cheers in years."

Duck gets the trophy.
Rooster fixes the machine.

Toucan sits down
for a warm-up preen.

With the first notes
he calls Duck to join in.

Forget karaoke,
let the real concert begin.